#40411
Easy

DATE DUE

AG 29 98	OCT 25 2014		
SE 06 98			
OC 05 98			
NO 18 98			
JA 27 99			
JUL 22 2002	DELETED		
JUN 25 2003			
DEC 30 2003			
SE 29 05			
MY 29 06			
AP 26 07			

No AR Pts.

E
Wal   Wallace, Karen
        My hen is dancing

THIS CANDLEWICK BOOK BELONGS TO:

_____

For Oscar Branson
K. W.
For Lynne
A. J.

Text copyright © 1993 by Karen Wallace
Illustrations copyright © 1993 by Anita Jeram

First U.S. paperback edition 1996

The Library of Congress has cataloged
the hardcover edition as follows:

Wallace, Karen.
My hen is dancing / by Karen Wallace ;
illustrated by Anita Jeram.—1st U.S. ed.
(Read and wonder books)
Summary: Recreates a hen's day in the farmyard as she eats,
keeps her feathers clean, and cares for her chicks. Includes
additional facts in the form of hand-lettered notes.
ISBN 1-56402-303-6 (hardcover)
1. Chickens—Juvenile literature. [1. Chickens.]
I. Jeram, Anita, ill. II. Title. III. Series: Read and wonder.
SF487.5.W34   1994
636.5—dc20   93-930

ISBN 1-56402-961-1 (paperback)

10 9 8 7 6 5 4 3 2 1

Printed in Hong Kong

This book was typeset in Calligraphic 810.
The pictures were done in watercolor and pen and ink.

Candlewick Press
2067 Massachusetts Avenue
Cambridge, Massachusetts 02140

My Hen Is Dancing

by
Karen Wallace

illustrated by
Anita Jeram

CANDLEWICK PRESS
CAMBRIDGE, MASSACHUSETTS

My hen is dancing
in the farmyard.

She takes two
steps forward

and one
step back.

She bends her neck and
pecks and scratches.

Her beak snaps shut.
She's found a worm.

A hen doesn't have teeth.
Food goes down into a pouch
in her body to be softened, and then
into her gizzard, where it's ground up
by the bits of grit she swallows.

My hen is rolling
in her dust bath.

She likes the ground
when it's gritty and dry.

Dust baths are good for cleaning
feathers and controlling fleas.

She cleans her feathers
with her beak and scratches
her ears with her toenails.

A hen also preens herself every day with oil.
It comes from where her tail feathers grow,
and she picks it up with her beak.

She stretches her wings
and sleeps in the sun.

My hen never struggles
if you hold her.

Her feathers are long
and smooth on her wings.

A hen can't fly far because her wings aren't strong but she can flutter up and down from a perch.

Underneath she's soft
like a feather duster.
Her bones feel hard
like thin sticks inside her.

My hen lives in a henhouse
with five other hens.

There's fresh straw on the floor

and a row
of nestboxes
along the
back wall.

A rooster lives there too. He has shiny tail feathers and a red coxcomb like a crown.

If my hen wanders,
he brings her home.

My hen lays big brown eggs.
When there are chicks
growing inside them,
she sits in her nest box
and puffs up her feathers.

She pecks you if you try
to touch them.

Some kinds of hens lay brown eggs.
Some kinds of hens lay white eggs.
No kind of hen lays both.

A hen's chicks take three weeks to hatch.
She sits on the eggs, turning them every
day so that they stay warm all over.

While she is sitting on her eggs,
she is called a "broody" hen.

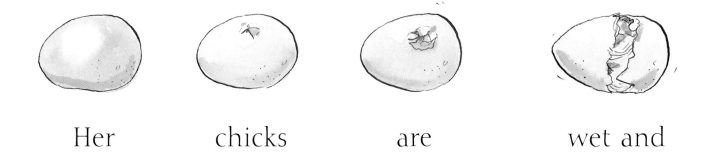

Her   chicks   are   wet and

They creep underneath her

sticky   when they   hatch.

A newborn chick
needs the warmth
of its mother to
survive.

where she's fluffy and warm.

My hen leads her chicks around the farmyard.

They learn to scratch and peck

and pull worms from the ground.

It takes about six months for a
chick to grow into a hen or a rooster.

My hen knows when it's time to go to sleep.
As soon as it gets dark, she hops
into the henhouse.

She sleeps standing up.
Her long toes grip
the perch so she
doesn't fall.

Sleeping like this is called "roosting."

We close the henhouse door at night
to keep her safe from hungry foxes.

In the morning I open the door. The rooster
jumps out with my hen close behind him.

The rooster crows, and
she steps up beside him.

Hens eat all kinds of things, including corn,
crumbs, worms, insects, grass, and vegetable scraps.

My hen is dancing
in the farmyard.

The hens in this book are so busy! When they bustle around it's as if they're dancing.

KAREN WALLACE, the author of *Think of an Eel* and *Think of a Beaver,* two more books in the Read and Wonder series, grew up in a log cabin in Quebec. She says that after keeping hens for as long as she has, you really get to know them. "When they peck and scratch, they really do seem to be dancing."

ANITA JERAM has illustrated many books for children, including the best-selling *Guess How Much I Love You* by Sam McBratney, *Dick King-Smith's Animal Friends,* and *All Pigs Are Beautiful,* also by Dick King-Smith. She is the author-illustrator of *Contrary Mary, Daisy Dare,* and *The Most Obedient Dog in the World.* "Illustrating *My Hen Is Dancing* appealed to me because it's about hens living the kind of life that all hens should live," she says. "I hope the book will help readers see them the way I see them."